How It's Done

Making a Book

by Wendy Hinote Lanier

FOCUS READERS

BEACON

www.focusreaders.com

Focus Readers is distributed by North Star Editions:
sales@northstareditions.com | 888-417-0195

Produced for Focus Readers by Red Line Editorial.

Content Consultant: Brienna Rossiter, Editor, Red Line Editorial

Photographs ©: Jello5700/iStockphoto, cover, 1; FangXiaNuo/iStockphoto, 4; George Rudy/Shutterstock Images, 7; m-imagephotography/iStockphoto, 8, 29; Zephyr18/iStockphoto, 11; andresr/iStockphoto, 13; kupicoo/iStockphoto, 14–15; GaudiLab/Shutterstock Images, 17; Lamaip/iStockphoto, 19; Dea/G. Dagli Ortoi/De Agostini/Getty Images, 21; RapidEye/iStockphoto, 22; Moreno Soppelsa/Shutterstock Images, 25; Red Line Editorial, 27

Library of Congress Cataloging-in-Publication Data
Names: Hinote Lanier, Wendy, 1963- author.
Title: Making a book / by Wendy Hinote Lanier.
Description: Lake Elmo , MN : Focus Readers, 2020. | Series: How it's done | Includes index. | Audience: Grades 4–6
Identifiers: LCCN 2019032154 (print) | LCCN 2019032155 (ebook) | ISBN 9781644930380 (hardcover) | ISBN 9781644931172 (paperback) | ISBN 9781644932759 (ebook pdf) | ISBN 9781644931967 (hosted ebook)
Subjects: LCSH: Bookbinding--Juvenile literature. | Book design--Juvenile literature.
Classification: LCC Z271 .H66 2020 (print) | LCC Z271 (ebook) | DDC 686.3--dc23
LC record available at https://lccn.loc.gov/2019032154
LC ebook record available at https://lccn.loc.gov/2019032155

Printed in the United States of America
Mankato, MN
012020

About the Author

Wendy Hinote Lanier is a former elementary teacher and a Texan through and through. She writes and speaks for children and adults on a variety of topics. She is the author of more than 40 books for children and young adults on topics related to science, technology, social studies, the arts, and, of course, Texas.

Table of Contents

Chapter 1

At the Library

The library buzzes with quiet activity. People wander up and down the rows. The smell of books fills the air. People study the book covers and titles. They choose books to check out.

People can find books to read at the library.

Some of the books are **nonfiction**. They tell about things that really happened. They tell about facts. Other books are **fiction**. The authors made up the stories. The stories are not completely true.

All of the books have one thing in common. They all began with

Fun Fact

The US Library of Congress is the world's largest library. It has more than 164 million items.

At bookstores and libraries, books are organized by type or topic.

an idea. But there are many steps between an idea and a finished book.

Chapter 2

Big Ideas

Ideas for a book can come from anywhere. An author may see or read something interesting. Or an author may **brainstorm** ideas in a group or on his or her own. Some of the ideas are never developed.

Authors may think through many ideas before choosing one to write about.

But an author needs only one good idea for a book.

Next, the author decides what kind of book to write. For nonfiction books, authors **research** the topic. They look for facts to include in their books. For fiction books, authors decide who the characters are. They create stories. They decide what the characters will do.

Authors also decide who the audience will be. They decide if the books will be for children or

Nonfiction authors can read books or look online for facts.

adults. Children's books are written about topics that interest kids. They often include photos or drawings.

Adult books are about topics that interest adults. All books fit into categories called genres. For example, some books are about mysteries. Others are about made-up worlds.

Authors often create outlines before they start writing. An outline is a way to plan out a book. The

Fun Fact

In Iceland, people often give books to one another during the holiday season.

Different authors use different tools for organizing their thoughts.

author lists the key points in the book. The author also decides the order of those points. Outlines help authors see what is missing in their work. Outlines prepare authors to write a full draft.

Chapter 3

The Writing Process

With a plan in place, the author begins writing. Some authors prefer to work on the computer. Others write by hand. Authors may work at home. Or they may write in a coffee shop or park.

Many authors have a specific place where they work best.

Some books take only a short time to write. Others can take months or years. It depends on the type of book being written. But the completed book is only a **rough draft**. There is still more work to do.

Authors send their drafts to **editors**. Editors read the drafts.

Fun Fact

The first printed books were made in China. They were printed approximately 1,200 years ago using wooden plates.

Editors and authors work together to make books better.

They give notes about how to improve the text. They suggest ways to make the writing clearer.

Using this feedback, authors rewrite parts of their books. They make changes based on their editors' suggestions. Then they send the books to their editors again. A book often goes back and forth several times. The author and the editor work together. They want the book to be the best it can be.

Fun Fact

The first electronic book was uploaded to the internet in 1971. It was a copy of the US Declaration of Independence.

A proofreader points out any errors in the book.

When the book's **content** is set, it goes to a copy editor and a **proofreader**. These people have not read the book yet. They look for spelling and **punctuation** errors. They correct any mistakes. When they finish, the book is ready for production.

THAT'S AMAZING!

The World's Oldest Book

Not everyone agrees on what makes a book. For this reason, the world's oldest book is hard to prove. But people do agree that books have been around a very long time.

The world's oldest book may be one found in Bulgaria. It has six pages held together by wire rings. The pages are made of gold plates. The plates show several figures. And they have letters no one today can understand.

A man found the book during the building of a canal. He gave it to a museum. The book is thought to be more than 2,500 years old.

The oldest book may have been similar to this gold plate.

STICKERS
Palace Pets
STICKER BOOK
TREASURY
First Sticker Activity Book
Disney
FROZEN
Disney
FAIRIES
THOMAS & FRIENDS
All Aboard!
My First
Sticker Book
Press-out rocket
over 50 reusable stickers
Roaring
Rockets
Activity Book
ACTIVITY Collection
Read and Create
THOMAS & FRIENDS
A Race to

Chapter 4

Book Production

The edited book goes to a design team. Designers create the book's layout and design. They plan how the book will look. They place photos or artwork. And they design the book's cover.

Some books include interesting features such as activity pages.

Designers and editors work for a publisher. This company creates a **proof** of the book for review. The author and editors check the proof. They examine the art or photos. Editors proofread the book again. They make changes to the text and images if needed.

Fun Fact

Publishers may hire artists to draw pictures for the book. Or they may purchase photos.

The printer creates a printing plate from a computer file.

When everyone is satisfied, the book is ready for manufacture. The final computer file is sent to the printer. The file includes all text, art, and photos. From the file, the printer creates large sheets called plates. Each plate holds 32 or 64 pages of the book.

The plates are put on the press machine. A roller transfers the images on the plates to paper. The newly printed sheet is called a signature. A machine folds the signatures so that the pages appear in the correct order. The machine sews the pages in the book together. It trims the edges. Finally, it adds the book's cover.

The book that began as an idea is now complete. Finished books go to the publisher. The publisher

MANUFACTURING A BOOK

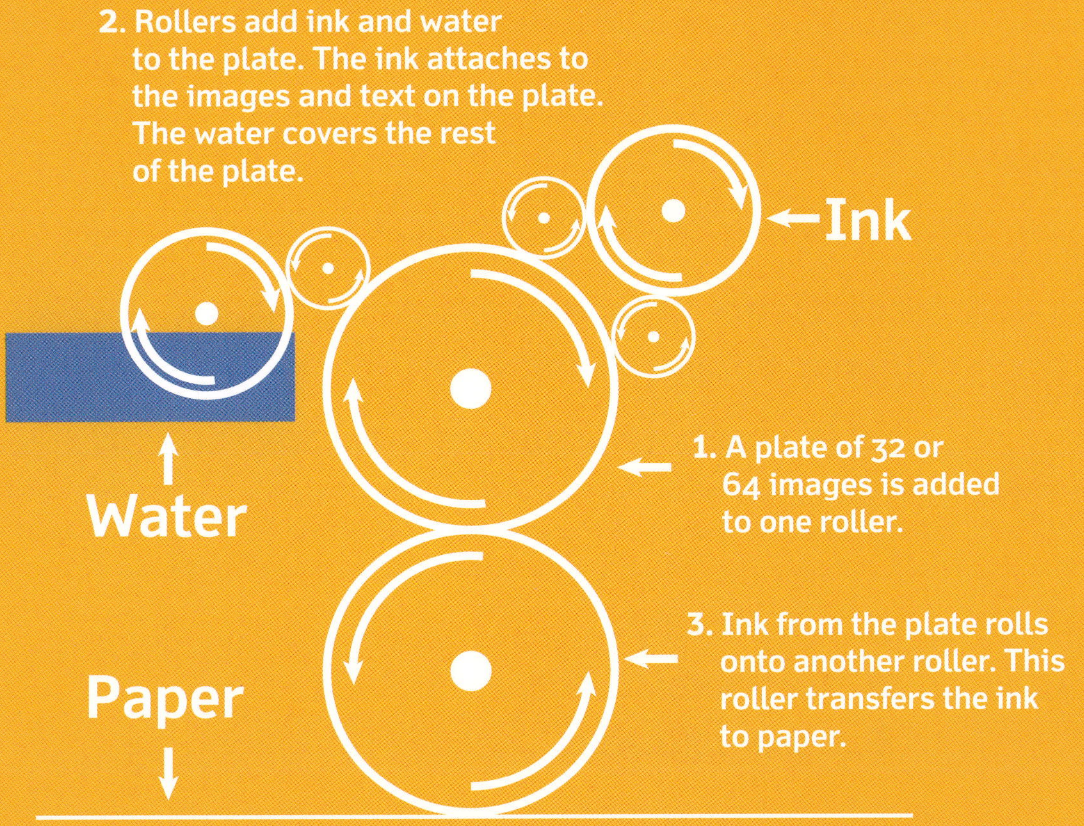

sends the new books to booksellers. Soon the new books are in the hands of readers.

FOCUS ON

Making a Book

Write your answers on a separate piece of paper.

1. Write a letter to a friend describing the different people who work on a book.
2. What kind of book would you want to write? Why?
3. Who reads the book for punctuation errors?
   - **A.** the publisher
   - **B.** the printer
   - **C.** the proofreader
4. What do the layout and design of a book do?
   - **A.** They make the book thicker.
   - **B.** They give the book a clear topic.
   - **C.** They determine how the book will look.

5. What does **manufacture** mean in this book?

*When everyone is satisfied, the book is ready for **manufacture**. The final computer file is sent to the printer.*

- **A.** construction
- **B.** writing
- **C.** review

6. What does **audience** mean in this book?

*Authors also decide who the **audience** will be. They decide if the books will be for children or adults.*

- **A.** the topic or category of a book
- **B.** the people who will read a book
- **C.** the people who will edit a book

Answer key on page 32.

Glossary

brainstorm
To get new ideas by considering all possibilities and letting thoughts flow freely.

content
The information or subject matter of a book.

editors
People responsible for developing books to be printed.

fiction
Books that describe made-up people or events.

nonfiction
Books that describe real facts, people, or events.

proof
An early version of a book created to check the images and text.

proofreader
A person who makes note of errors in a written document.

punctuation
Marks used in writing to separate parts of sentences or make the meaning clear.

research
To study something to learn more about it.

rough draft
The first version of a written document.

To Learn More

BOOKS

Cameron, Neill. *How to Make Awesome Comics.* New York: Scholastic, 2017.

Deutsch, Libby. *Everyday Journeys of Ordinary Things.* Tulsa, OK: EDC Publishing, 2019.

Ruzicka, Oldrich. *How Things Are Made.* New York: Sterling Children's Books, 2016.

NOTE TO EDUCATORS

Visit **www.focusreaders.com** to find lesson plans, activities, links, and other resources related to this title.

Index

Answer Key: 1. Answers will vary; **2.** Answers will vary; **3.** C; **4.** C; **5.** A; **6.** B